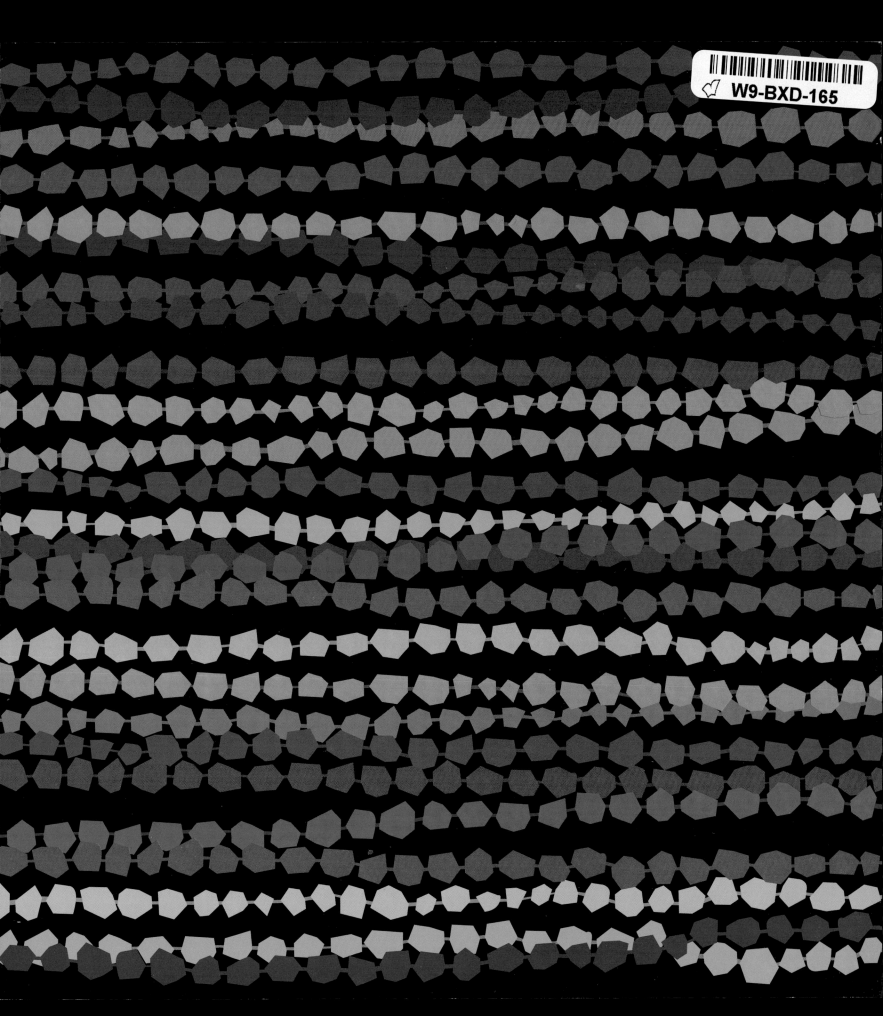

For Martha,
salsa dancer extraordinaire,
whose dancing is always inspiring.
—D. A.

In loving memory
of Honey, our grandmother,
who taught us all to dance
and in whose world
nobody was ever too big
to dance, even Mrs. Granger
and her watermelon pickles.

And for Donna Jean who
loved to play the banjo
and dance to Dudley.
—S. A.

DANCE TONITE

CIP Data is available
Published in the United States in 2004 by Handprint Books
413 Sixth Avenue
Brooklyn, New York 11215
www.handprintbooks.com
First Edition
ISBN: 1-59354-046-9

Printed in China
2 4 6 8 10 9 7 5 3 1

TOO BIG
TO DANCE

Story by Doug Anderson

Illustrated by Sara Anderson

A Crawdad County Book

Way back in the bayou country lies Crawdad County. The Spanish moss on the live oaks hangs so thick that unless you look especially closely, you might not notice rickety Alligator Acres, huddled cozily upon the water's edge. It's country just teeming with folks, a friendly kind of place Cecil, the alligator, calls home.

Back beyond live Cecil's neighbors, including little Woo, the armadillo, and a zebra named Eloise. Just how a zebra came to be there is a story for another time. The wind does not often blow through the steamy bayou—but when it does, a story is sure to follow. The wind is blowing tonight, there's a distant fiddle singing, and the story we are here to tell is about the Crawdad County dance—of Eloise, who didn't quite fit in, and of Cecil and Woo, who made sure that she did.

Cecil, gracious gator,
      heard the wind come singing,
Wishing it would take his cares
      and with them go a-winging.

Woo, the armadillo, settled in the grassy wind,
Hoping something nice might happen to a little guy like him.

A wind came on the bayou, distant stars began to rise.
Sweet Eloise, the zebra, got some stardust in her eyes.

Dreaming of the evening, anticipating fun.

They talk as they await the setting of the sun.

Cecil, Woo, and Eloise are stepping out tonight.
Across the beaten bayou path, southern stars are smiling bright.

A breeze was in the bayou, it was a night to take a chance,
For all who had their hearts set on the Crawdad County dance.

Spirits were rising levee high, as the three friends came to town.
Lights were strung at the Laissez Faire, fiddles sang a Cajun sound.

Laughs spilled deep into the night, music spread far and wide.
Cecil and Woo and some turtles, too, made their way inside.

Inside, Cecil dos-a-doed, while Woo was whisked and whirled.

Some danced stately, solemn, and straight—others tossed and twirled.

Eloise walked up to the door, her heart set on romance.

But she could not reach the hardwood floor, she was too big to dance.

While down below the dance went on, her heart was feeling blue.

Woo was whirling once around, when he chanced a glance outdoors.

Where he saw sweet Eloise, swaying sadly on all fours.

Armadillo hearts are precious things, they feel deeper than the river.

Wistful Woo walked from the dance to spend a moment with her.

Cecil swung and Cecil stomped, to the drumming beat until,
He missed his little armadillo friend, and saw him standing on the hill

Clever Cecil grabbed a squeeze box as the band behind him played.

Then out to Woo and Eloise, he led a dance parade.

So they all waltzed slow together, as the moon shone on the pond.
Large and little they did dance, as the band played "Jolie Blonde."

When the music is over in Crawdad County, when the dance is done,
There are still some stars to steal our hearts, on the other side of the sun

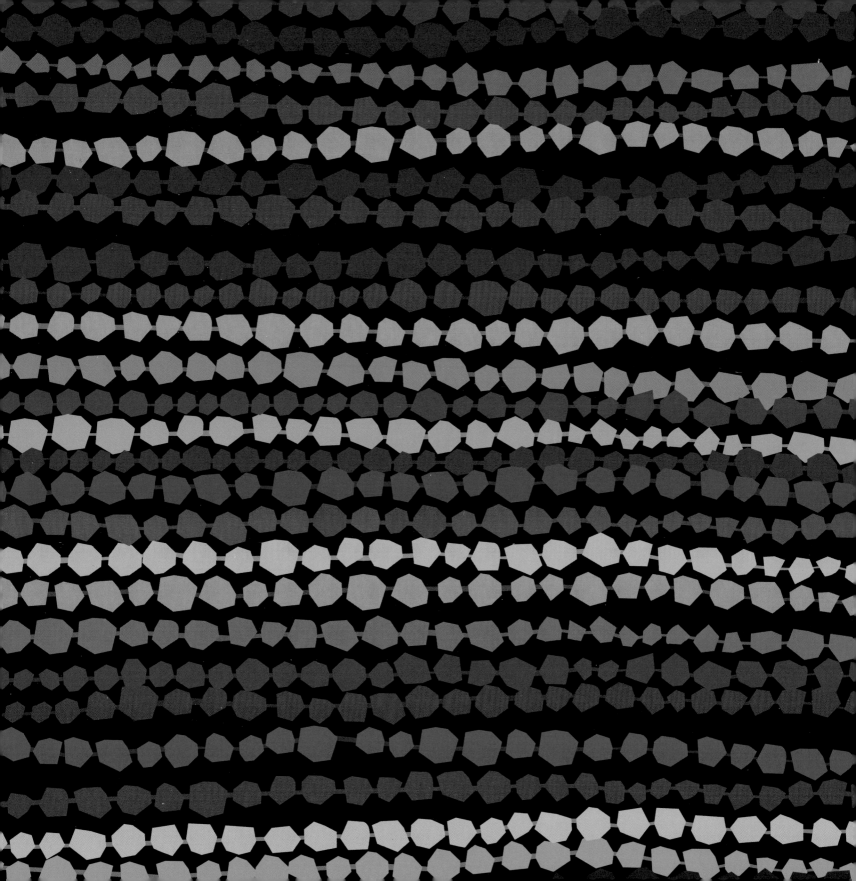